WALT DISNEY'S

Cinderella

WALT DISNEY'S
Cinderella

Jaq Saves the Day

Adaptation by Emily Stewart

DISNEY
PRESS

New York

WALT DISNEY'S
Cinderella

Jaq Saves the Day

Chapter One

Mice for Breakfast

*J*ust because you're small doesn't mean you can't be a big help. Take me, Jaq. Some might call me a mouse. Well, I *am* a mouse. But that doesn't mean I'm not an important part of this story!

I'm the one who met Cinderelly first. It was the very first night her stepmother ordered Cinderelly to move upstairs to the attic. Cinderelly had to leave her big, sunny bedroom and move into the damp, dark space. How Cinderelly cried that night! It broke my heart.

She cried because she missed her father. He died when Cinderelly was still a little girl. He only married her stepmother because he thought his daughter needed a woman's care. He didn't know that his new wife had a cold heart.

That first night, Cinderelly sobbed into her thin pillow. I peeked out of my mouse-hole and tiptoed across the dusty floor. And when a mouse tiptoes, he's *quiet*. I sat right on her pillow. I wanted to comfort her, but I didn't know how.

Well, Cinderelly turned and saw me. I expected her to scream, the way people do. You should see her stepsisters run when they

see me! But instead, she smiled. Your heart can crack at a smile like that.

She picked me up in the palm of her hand. "You're awfully cute, little mouse," she said. "Have you come to comfort me?"

"Yes!" I squeaked. "Don't cry." She didn't understand me. Not then. It took her a little while to under- stand how mice talk. But when I softly patted her finger, she smiled again. We've been friends ever since.

On the morning that my story really begins, everything seemed to happen at once. Cinderelly had overslept.

"I had the most wonderful dream!" she told the birds who wake her each morning.

But there was no time for dreaming. Stepmother is fierce if Cinderelly is late with the breakfast trays! We helped her get dressed. But we had one problem. A new mouse had been caught in one of Stepmother's traps. I convinced the plump mouse that we all just wanted to be friends. We little guys have to stick together!

Cinderelly freed him with gentle hands. She named him Gus and gave him a shirt and cap. The shirt was a little too tight, but

our Cinderelly didn't have time to make a new one.

Then it was time for break-fast. Every morning, Cinderelly feeds the hens and chickens. She makes sure to scatter extra corn just for us.

But this morning, we ran into a little problem. Well, a *big* problem. Lucifer.

Most cats don't scare me. But Lucifer does. He's the meanest, most terrible cat in the world. He has the sharpest teeth and claws . . . and he likes to use them on tiny mice.

We had to tip-toe past him. But he opened one lazy green eye and saw us. We ran for our lives! But greedy Gus had tried to carry too

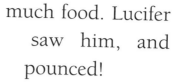

much food. Lucifer saw him, and pounced!

Gus had to hide under a teacup. I didn't see him in time. But I *did* see Cinderelly scoop up the tray. She headed upstairs to her stepsisters' rooms.

Uh-oh! Trouble!

Chapter Two

The King Gives a Ball

$\mathcal{I}$ dived into a mouse-hole, swung my way up a spiderweb, and scampered up a wall. But I was still too late.

"You did that on purpose!" Drizella screeched. A broken teacup lay smashed on the floor. Gus had already dived behind a curtain.

"But—" Cinderelly started.

"Moth-er!" Drizella cried. She wiped at the place on her cheek where a tear would be, if she had the heart to cry. "Cinderella is sooo mean!"

I hid behind a curtain as Stepmother gave Cinderelly a list of extra duties to perform. Wash the linen sheets and iron them! Clean the windows! Polish the silver! Scrub the hallway!

Poor Cinderelly!

We watched sadly as she went about her chores. But Cinderelly soon grew cheerful. She began to sing as she scrubbed the stone floor. We all gathered close to listen.

Then, we heard a knock at the front door. Cinderelly went to answer it. A footman from

the royal palace handed her an envelope.

It was an invitation to a ball. And every young woman in the kingdom was invited.

"That means *I* can go!" Cinderelly cried.

Drizella and Anastasia hooted with laughter. "You!" they cried. "Go to a ball? Will you take your broom?"

But Stepmother looked down her nose. "Yes, you can go, Cinderella," she said. She spoke in a fake-sweet voice that meant trouble. "*If* you finish your work. And *if* you have a suitable dress to wear."

Cinderelly broke out into a smile. "Thank you, Stepmother!" she cried.

The other mice danced with glee. But I didn't trust Cinderelly's stepmother. She had something up her sleeve.

Which meant Cinderelly might need our help.

Chapter Three

Preparations

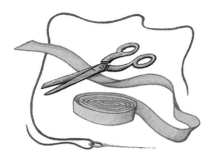

I was right. Cinderelly's stepmother did have an evil plan. She kept Cinderelly busy all day long.

She had to find ribbon, lace, and jewelry. She had to sew ruffles and iron gowns. She was ordered to fluff petticoats and smooth wrinkles.

She didn't have a minute to herself. But I, Jaq, knew this would happen. And I had a plan.

While Cinderelly worked, her attic friends worked, too! Cinderelly had an old gown that had belonged to her mother. It was a little shabby. But it just needed some help to be beautiful.

Gus and I sneaked through the house and found beads and lace that the step-sisters had thrown away. The birds and mice busily sewed and arranged until Cinderelly's old gown was like new.

At the end of the day, we heard

Cinderelly's tired step. She looked so sad as she came inside.

"There will be other balls," she whispered. She was trying to be brave. But then, she burst into tears.

That's when the birds opened her closet door, and her beautiful gown was revealed.

"It's perfect!" Cinderelly cried.

In only seconds, she was dressed and ready. She hurried downstairs to catch her stepsisters and stepmother.

"Oh, please wait for me!" she called.

Stepmother stopped. She was shocked that Cinderelly had been able to dress in a beautiful gown. Not only that, Cinderelly looked a hundred times prettier than Stepmother's daughters.

The corners of her thin, mean lips turned down. "What a pretty gown," she said in a voice like sour milk. She fingered a piece of the lace we'd taken from Drizella's wastebasket. "And look how nicely you've trimmed it."

"Wait a minute—that's mine!" Drizella screeched.

"And those beads are *mine!*" Anastasia shrieked.

The two girls tore at Cinderelly's gown.

They snatched the beads from around her neck. Soon, her beautiful dress was in tatters.

Stepmother shook her head. "Well, you certainly can't go to a ball looking like *that*," she said. "Come, girls!"

And they swept out the door.

Chapter Four

Surprises and Fairy Dust

Cinderelly ran into the garden. She cried as though her heart would break. We all gathered around her. But we couldn't make her feel any better. We'd never seen her so heartbroken.

Gus looked up at the sky. He poked me. I

was about to pinch him back, but then I noticed something strange. Tiny sparkles were forming in the air! They went 'round and 'round, faster and faster. Suddenly, a lady with a rosy face appeared.

"Now, don't cry, dear," she said. "You can't go to a ball with a red nose, can you?"

Cinderelly wiped her eyes. "B-but I'm not going to the ball. And who are you?"

Cinderella didn't mean to be rude. But it was funny to find a stranger in your very own garden. No matter how kind she might appear.

The woman frowned as she looked around the garden. "I need a pumpkin."

"A . . . pumpkin?" Cinderelly repeated.

"Yes, it's a large, round orange squash—"

"I know what a pumpkin

is," Cinderelly said kindly. "I just don't—"

"Good! Then you can fetch one!"

The woman said this with such a happy smile that Cinderelly sprang up and fetched a pumpkin from the patch.

"Splendid! That will do!" The woman reached out her hand, and a wand appeared in the air, just like that! She waved it and said some strange words. They sounded like *bibbidi bobbidi boo*, if you can believe that.

Then, the pumpkin turned into a beautiful carriage!

Cinderelly gasped. She turned to the stranger. "Why, you must be—"

"Your fairy godmother, dear. No time to chat, we need some mice," the fairy god-mother said cheerfully.

Now, usually, when a person is looking for mice, I dive for the nearest mouse-hole. But I knew this lady would help Cinderelly. I

darted forward, with a couple of my friends. Then I ran back and tugged Gus forward, too.

The fairy godmother waved her wand over us. What happened next was the strangest thing of all. First, my nose started to itch. Then, my legs started to tingle. And my tail suddenly grew thick and silky. I became a horse!

Let me tell you, I am a handsome mouse. But I was a *magnificent* horse. I pranced and preened for Cinderelly.

"Oh, my goodness!" she laughed.

In a twinkling, the fairy godmother had changed the old barnyard horse into a dashing coachman. Bruno the dog became a footman.

But she saved the best for last. With a wave of her wand, Cinderelly's tattered dress became a beautiful gown. It sparkled and shone in the moonlight. And on her tiny feet were a pair of sparkling glass slippers.

"No time to tarry— must go," the fairy godmother warned as Cinderelly climbed into the carriage. "Oh, and remember this—it's very important. The spell will be broken on the stroke of twelve midnight. Do you hear?"

"Midnight," Cinderelly repeated. "I'll remember."

The coachman cracked his whip in the air. We lifted our strong, graceful legs. The weight of the carriage was no heavier than a feather. We were off for the palace!

Chapter Five

The Grandest Ball of All

We watched Cinderelly walk slowly up the stairs to the palace. She seemed a little frightened. You would be, too. The palace was so grand, and the soldiers looked so fierce! I tossed my head and whinnied to give her courage.

Although I enjoyed my silky mane and my graceful legs, I wished I were a mouse again. Then I could sneak into the palace and see what was going on.

But Bruno the coachman signaled us. He'd spied a window looking into the ballroom. We all crept over to peek inside.

We saw the prince take Cinderelly's hand. They looked into each other's eyes. And they began to dance.

They danced and danced, all evening long. The prince never looked at another girl. He kept Cinderelly's hand tucked into his. They spoke to each other softly, and sometimes they laughed. They only had eyes for each other.

Then Gus grew restless. He tossed his head toward the big clock on the tower and whinnied. I looked at the clock with a start. It was almost midnight!

Cinderelly was still dancing with the prince. Her head rested against his shoulder. We tried to signal her, but her eyes were closed.

And then the clock began to chime. *Bong! Bong!*

Cinderelly dropped the prince's hand. She hurried away. We all scrambled to get back to the palace steps. *Bong! Bong!* pealed the clock.

We were ready and pawing the ground when Cinderelly flew out of the palace. The prince ran behind her, trying to catch up. One of Cinderelly's slippers fell off, but she kept on running. *Bong! Bong! Bong!* She jumped inside the carriage. *Bong!*

We took off at a fast gallop. Behind us, the king's men chased us on their fastest horses. My ears rang from the noise of the chimes. *Bong! Bong! Bong!* My lungs felt like they were going to burst.

Then the last *bong* sounded. My legs began to tingle again. My nose itched. I shrank, and I was Jaq the mouse again. The carriage was a pumpkin. Cinderelly was in rags.

One of her feet was bare. And the other still wore a glass slipper.

Chapter Six

The Glass Slipper

*Y*ou'd think that Cinderelly would be sad the next day. But she went around with a happy smile on her face.

"I had a dream come true," she told us softly. "Thanks to my fairy godmother!"

Then we heard amazing news. The prince

had fallen in love with the girl he'd danced with at the ball! He still had her glass slipper. Every young woman would have a chance to try it on. If it fit, he would take that woman as his bride.

Cinderelly's stepsisters hopped about with glee. They were sure they had a chance to win the prince. Cinderelly blushed, and I saw her stepmother frown as she watched her.

Everyone left to put on their prettiest dresses. I tried to run upstairs to warn Cinderelly. But it was too late. Stepmother had locked her inside her room!

"Please, you must let me out!" she cried.

But Stepmother dropped the key in her pocket and walked away laughing.

Now it was time for the mice to save the day. Gus and I ran downstairs. We never took our eyes off Stepmother's pocket.

The grand duke arrived with the glass slipper. Anastasia and Drizella both tried to force their big feet into the tiny slipper.

But while Stepmother watched her

daughters, we climbed into her pocket and stole the key!

We raced back up to the attic. We pushed the key under the door to Cinderelly, and she unlocked the door. "Hurry!" we urged her.

It seemed to take forever to run back downstairs. When we burst into the room, Stepmother was just telling the grand duke that  there were no other young ladies in the house.

"Please wait, Your Grace," Cinderelly said. "May I try?"

But Stepmother had one more evil trick. She tripped the grand duke as he headed toward Cinderelly. The glass slipper smashed into a million pieces!

But Cinderelly took the other slipper out

of her pocket. The duke held it out, and she slipped her foot into it. It fit perfectly.

You can imagine the rest. How happy the prince was when he found her. How Cinderelly found her true love. She'll make a perfect queen.

And you should have seen how

Stepmother stamped her foot as Cinderelly became the prince's bride!

All of Cinderelly's friends were at the wedding, of course. We watched her drive away in a beautiful carriage. Bells were ringing and the sun was shining, and she was happy at last.

Do you wonder what happened to me, Jaq, the hero of this story? I'll tell you—palace life is wonderful!

Meet the Disney Girls!

Ella, Ariel, Isabelle, Jasmine, Yukiko, and Paula.
They're more than just best friends—they're Disney
Girls! Each girl shares special qualities with a Disney
Princess—and sometimes, the girls even become those
princesses. With best friends like these and a touch of
magic, dreams really can come true!

One of Us
Available now

Attack of the Beast
Available now

**And Sleepy
Makes Seven**
Available now

A Fish Out of Water
Available now

Cinderella's Castle
Available now

One Pet Too Many
Available
January 1999

**Adventure in
Walt Disney World**
Available March 1999

Read all the books in the series.
Look for more books next spring and summer.

Experience all the fun of Walt Disney World "Olsen" style

Mary Kate & Ashley's Walt Disney World Adventure

ISBN 0-7868-3205-3 $14.95

Available in September

ALSO LOOK FOR:

Once Upon a Time with Mary Kate & Ashley:
A Disney Princess Story and Activity Collection

ISBN 0-7868-3189-8 $16.95

Available now

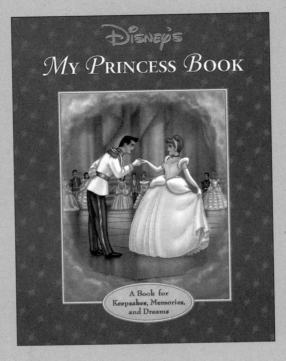